To Hannah Ray and to all children who make new discoveries about the
ocean and its creatures. —L.T.

To Dr. Richard Rosenblatt and the crew of the Scripps Institution Marine Vertebrate Collection,
who opened the doors of their collection and shared their knowledge with me. —N.W.

Cover and book design by Carrie Leeb, Leeb & Sons.

Typeset in Clarendon and Trade Gothic.

Printed in Hong Kong.

Library of Congress Cataloging-in-Publication Data

Taylor, Leighton R.

Creeps from the deep : life in the deep sea / text by Leighton Taylor ; photographs by Norbert Wu.

p.   cm.

Includes index.

Summary: In text and photographs, presents what is known about the deep ocean and the exotic creatures that live there.

ISBN: 0-8118-1297-9

1. Deep-sea biology--Juvenile literature. 2. Deep-sea animals--Juvenile literature. [1. Marine biology. 2. Marine animals. 3. Ocean.] I. Wu, Norbert, ill.
II. Title.

QH91.16.T38   1997

578.77'7--dc21   97-4081
                                                  CIP
                                                  AC

Distributed in Canada by Raincoast Books

8680 Cambie Street

Vancouver

British Columbia V6P 6M9

10 9 8 7 6 5 4 3 2 1

Chronicle Books

85 Second Street

San Francisco

California 94105

Website: www.chronbooks.com

Creeps from the Deep

By Leighton Taylor Photographed by Norbert Wu

chronicle books · san francisco

Table of Contents

Deep-sea Submersible

Deep-sea
Swallower

Juvenile Fangtooth

What's It Like Down There?

Imagine living in the deep sea. It's freezing cold. It's dark. Food is scarce. Tons of water push down on and sweep across the ocean floor. Life in the deep sea is very different from life on land.

Far below the sunlit surface live some of Earth's weirdest creatures. There are squids that squirt clouds of light, silver-bodied hatchetfish shaped like tiny ax blades, snaky black devilfish with fangs as long as their tails, bright red worms ten feet tall, and fat female anglerfish with fishing poles and glowing lures. Who knows what else waits to be found?

In the dark, cold world of the deep, things are very different from our world on land. Landscapes at the bottom of the sea are more extreme than landscapes above sea level. In some places the ocean floor is flat and muddy, in others, steep and rocky. And in some places, boiling water gushes from volcanic vents on the ocean floor.

Seawater is also much heavier than air on land and moves with much greater force. It takes a strong wind to blow your hat off, but even a small wave at the beach can knock you down. Great masses of seawater, called currents, move through the deep sea. Currents can move very slowly or at speeds faster than many animals can swim. In some deep places the ocean is still and barely moves.

These vast dark spaces and cold rugged landscapes of the deep sea are a challenge to life. It is here we find the oddly shaped and strangely adapted sea creatures, the creeps from the deep. Scientists continue to explore these vast and different places of the sea where creeps live. Much of what we know about strange deep-sea creatures and their distant

On dark nights, this baby sailfish shares the upper layers of the open sea with deep water animals that swim toward the surface to feed.

world has been discovered only in the past fifty years. Great discoveries will be made in the next twenty years. Maybe you will be one of the people to make them.

This view of the fangtooth may be the last that many deep-sea fish and small shrimp ever see. (In fact they may never see this in the deep-sea darkness, but they may feel those teeth.)

How Deep Is Deep?

This sub can withstand
hundreds of pounds of pressure.

Before we can really know the creeps of the deep, we need to look in more detail at what the deep sea is like. "How deep is deep?" you ask. Well, it all depends on your point of view. If you can't swim, water five feet deep can seem very deep. A snorkeler with really good lungs can hold her breath long enough to dive 70 feet down into the ocean. But when it's

150 feet to the bottom, that's very deep water for a swimmer. A scuba diver with compressed air in her tank can dive safely (if she follows all the rules) to almost 200 feet deep. With very special scuba diving gear, a diver can explore down to 500 feet. But to dive deeper than 500 feet, humans need to be inside pressurized containers like submarines or special diving suits made from strong incompressible materials like titanium and cast acrylic plastic. In deep water, we need protection from the icy water and intense pressure. Also, we need to take air with us so we can breathe and light so we can see.

Out of the water, we measure our distance above the surface of the sea in lengths of meters or feet called "altitude" or "elevation." In water, we call this measured distance "depth."

On land, it's easy for us to change our elevation. We can travel a long way by using a bicycle, car, bus, train, or even by walking. We can quickly go from a coastal town near sea level to high in the mountains. The elevator in a tall building can move us up from sea level to hundreds of feet higher in less than a minute. But in the ocean, even a short change in depth takes effort and equipment. Most people can walk to the store a mile away in twenty minutes. To go a mile deep in the sea is very difficult and few people have done it. It takes many days to

At about 40 feet down, this swimmer says good-bye to friends in the submersible. He ⋯▶ must return to the surface for air. In their air-filled and pressurized chamber, the sub riders can go to almost 3000 feet deep.

get ready for such a diving trip. You need a ship, a diving sub, and a large crew of people to help the divers in the sub. Most of the sea floor has never been seen by humans because undersea travel is made so difficult by pressure, cold, and darkness.

The deepest part of the ocean is in the Mariana Trench, near the Island of Guam. Here the water is more than 35,000 feet deep. That's almost seven miles below the sea surface and 6,000 feet deeper than Mount Everest is high. Two scientists visited here once in 1960 in a special diving chamber. It's time for somebody to go back.

MEASURING DISTANCE

The next time you pass a sign at the edge of a town or city, look at the numbers near the bottom of the sign. One number tells how many people live in the town. The other number tells the elevation, or the vertical distance of the town above sea level. In the United States, elevation is given in feet. In Canada and most other countries, it is measured in meters (1 meter = 3.28 feet).

Oh, the Pressure!

Living and moving in the sea is very different from living and moving on land because of all the water. Water is very dense compared to air. If you have ever tried to run in water about knee-deep you know that water is much thicker than air. In fact, seawater is about 800 times heavier than air. The weight of water causes the pressure in the ocean. Air on land has pressure too, but because air weighs much less than water, we can hardly feel it. A big reason that the deep sea is hard to visit is because of *pressure*, the force of tons of seawater pressing down.

For an idea of how scientists define pressure, try this. Lie down with your back on the ground, near sea level. Put a postage stamp on your forehead. Look up into the sky. Think about the piece of air that goes all the way from the stamp's surface to the place where space begins and there isn't any more air. The distance to that place is more than fifteen miles. You are lying at the bottom of an "ocean of air" that is more than 75,000 feet deep.

That fifteen-mile-long piece of air over the one-inch square on your forehead weighs only about fifteen pounds. Scientists call this weight on a surface of one inch at sea level "one atmosphere of pressure." As you go higher in elevation, say, from the seashore to a mountaintop, there is less air above you. That shorter piece of air over you weighs less, so the air pressure "atmospheric pressure" is lower.

The weight of water makes it difficult for people to explore the deep sea. Imagine a scuba diver in water 33 feet deep with a postage stamp on her forehead. The piece of water extending from her postage stamp to the sea surface weighs about 15 pounds! Water is so much heavier than air that 33 feet of seawater on a postage stamp weighs the same as 70,000 feet of air on the same sized stamp. Now imagine that the scuba diver swims down another 33

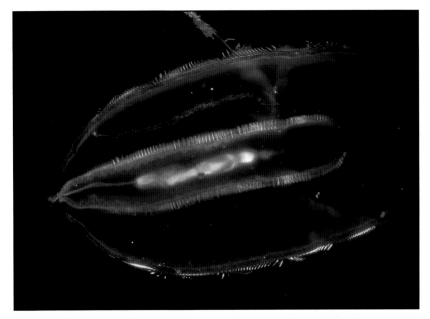

Comb jellies, their jellyfish relatives, and most marine animals have no air spaces in their bodies, so they can easily adjust to pressure changes.

feet. The weight of 66 feet of water is almost 30 pounds per square inch, or 2 atmospheres. For every 33 feet deeper the diver goes, she is under another atmosphere of pressure.

The deeper you go in the sea, the more pressure is on you. In the deepest part of the ocean, almost 35,000 feet down, water has a pressure of 16,000 pounds on every square inch. A school bus weighs about 16,000 pounds. Now that's seriously heavy pressure!

◄·······By taking along a supply of air, a scuba diver can stay down longer and deeper than a snorkeler can by breath-holding.

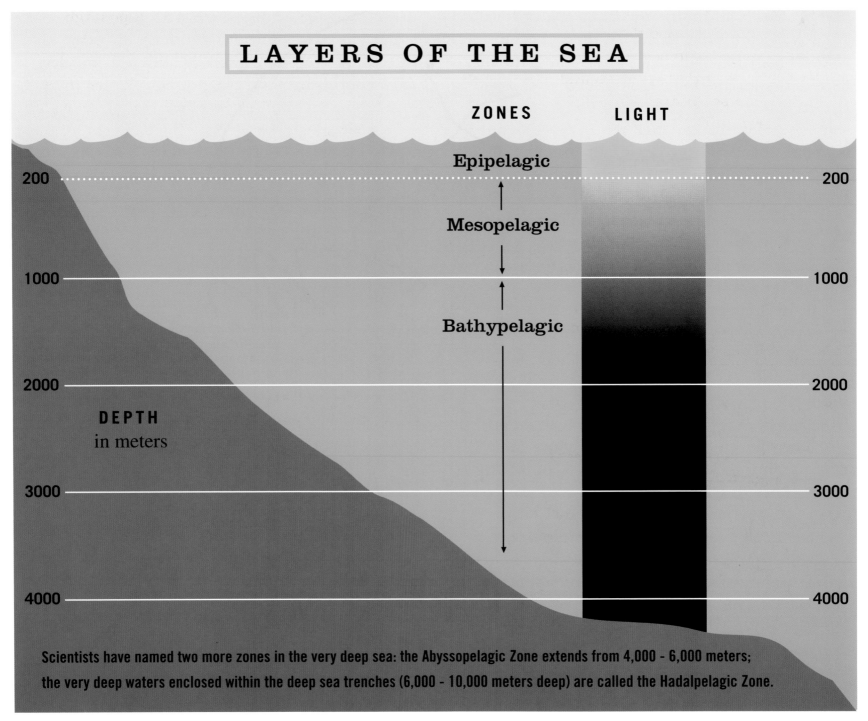

LAYERS OF THE SEA

ZONES

LIGHT

Epipelagic

200

Mesopelagic

1000

Bathypelagic

2000

DEPTH
in meters

3000

4000

Scientists have named two more zones in the very deep sea: the Abyssopelagic Zone extends from 4,000 - 6,000 meters; the very deep waters enclosed within the deep sea trenches (6,000 - 10,000 meters deep) are called the Hadalpelagic Zone.

Scientists divide the sea into four main layers. These are defined by depth, light, and whether or not they are on the bottom or in open water. The Epipelagic Zone is the light-filled layer near the surface. Beneath it is the Mesopelagic Zone; a layer far above the sea bottom and far below the surface. Below this middle layer is the always dark Bathypelagic Zone. The open water over the very deep bottom of the ocean is called the Benthopelagic Zone. The area right on the bottom is called the Benthic Zone.

When we look out over the open sea (which is also the very top of the epipelagic zone) it looks flat, ruffled only slightly by waves and wind. But the sea bottom is very different from place to place. Beneath the surface are huge mountains, deep canyons, vast plains, gaping trenches, and steep cliffs that drop for more than a mile. Try to visualize this gigantic underwater landscape that makes the mountains found on dry land seem tiny.

The ocean is deeper than the Earth's surface is high. At least one ocean trench is deeper than Earth's highest mountain is tall! Where

Blue sharks cruise the upper layers of open seas. They eat many things, including animals that migrate to the surface at night from deep water.

LAYERS OF THE SEA

Based on old words from Greek and Latin, the names for these layers tell us something about them, so it helps to learn the old words. You can recognize parts of the old words used in the modern names, which makes the modern names seem less difficult. Pelagios is an old Greek word for "open sea"; bathy means "deep"; epi means "upper"; meso means "middle"; benthos means "bottom."

Mount Everest stands 29,028 feet above sea level, the Mariana Trench, the deepest spot in the ocean, drops down to 36,201 feet below the surface of the sea. Deep ocean trenches are far longer and much deeper than any river-cut canyon on land, including Arizona's Grand Canyon. In some places, great expanses of flat mud on the seafloor stretch for great distances, making Africa's sandy Sahara Desert look like a park by comparison.

Imagine that some giant smoothed out all the mountains on dry land so everything was the same height. This "average height" would be just less than 3,000 feet above sea level. If the same giant hand smoothed the ocean basins to the same depth, the average depth would be a very deep 12,500 feet.

About 200 years ago, many scientists believed that there was no life in the sea deeper than 2,000 feet. Now we know they were wrong.

Early evidence of deep-sea animals was discovered accidentally about 150 years ago. A broken telegraph cable in the Mediterranean

Most of what we know about life in the deep sea has been learned by dragging or dropping nets and instruments from boats and ships.

Sea was retrieved from 7,000 feet down. Scientists were surprised to see animals such as worms, oysters, and scallops alive and growing on the cable.

Inspired by this enormous discovery of life in the deep sea, scientists planned the first big expedition to sail around the world to study the oceans. The expedition left from England in 1872 aboard the H.M.S. *Challenger*. Scientists dragged nets to catch animals, dropped weights on ropes to measure depth, measured the temperature and salt content of seawater, and scooped up mud from the bottom. The *Challenger* expedition made such exciting discoveries that more expeditions to study the deep sea were launched. Many things we know about the ocean and its creatures are from the books and pictures made by the scientists of the *Challenger*.

In the last thirty years many new tools to study the sea have been invented. But oceanographers, scientists who study the ocean, still use some devices similiar to the ones used on the *Challenger*. Long wires pull nets underwater to scoop up fish, jellyfish, sea stars, shrimps, and squid for study. Specimens are carefully preserved. They are labeled and kept in science museums so they can be studied. Such collections of specimens are like libraries. But instead of books, there are jars of wonderful animals hauled from the deep sea.

Many biologists prefer to study animals while the creatures are still living in their deep-sea homes, instead of looking at jars. In a way, relying only on netted specimens is like trying to learn about life in San Francisco by dragging nets from a blimp flying a half mile in the sky.

Visiting the deep sea has only recently become possible. William Beebe, one of this century's outstanding explorers, was the first person to dive into the deep sea and observe its creatures in their natural habitat. In 1934, Beebe led a shipboard expedition to the Atlantic Ocean off the island of Bermuda. On the deck of the ship, he crawled through a small hole into a thick steel ball, about five feet in diameter. The ball had walls 1 1/4 inches thick to withstand the pressure of the deep sea. A crane on the ship slowly lowered the ball over the side. Beebe called the big diving ball a "bathysphere," from *bathy* for "deep" and *sphere* for "ball." The bathysphere was lowered on steel cables almost 3,000 feet into the sea, deeper than anyone had ever gone before. Through a small, thick window made of quartz, William Beebe watched glowing animals that no one had ever seen alive.

Deep-diving research submersibles have since replaced Beebe's bathysphere. Their windows are made of the same thick, light plastic used to make the large windows in aquariums. Researchers dive many thousands of feet deep into the ocean riding in these pressurized, battery-powered subs. A ship on the surface launches the sub and stands by to help.

Some scientists prefer not to crawl into cramped subs. Instead, they stay aboard ships and send television cameras into the deep sea. These cameras are carried in special remote-controlled submarines lowered on cables. From the ship, scientists can watch televised pictures of living deep-sea creatures.

Deep Flight is a new kind of research sub. It can fly fast through the water. ······▶ Older subs, like *Alvin*, can take hours to reach the bottom as they must move slowly.

Life in the Deep

What do ocean-diving scientists see when they watch the animals that live there? Now that we know something about the living conditions in the deep sea, let's look at some of the many kinds of deep-sea creatures and consider how they live.

Remember that creeps of the deep live in a very different kind of world from the land where humans roam. We live on the hard bottom of a great sea of air called the atmosphere. Mostly we move in two directions—right and left, or back and forth. We are almost always moving on a surface.

Some creeps of the deep also live on surfaces, such as the rocks, sand, or mud of the sea bottom. But most of them live in the great open space of the sea, without walls or ceilings or floors. They move as easily up and down as they do back and forth. They move in three dimensions.

Humans only move freely in two dimensions. Sure, a pole-vaulter, or a skydiver, or a bungee jumper seem to move up and down, but they are really falling. Airplane pilots, hang gliders, and parasailors can move in all directions, but they need wings to do it. Only snorkelers and scuba divers can move easily in all three dimensions.

Animals in the ocean truly live in three dimensions. They move back and forth, up and down. Some animals—fish, squid, and shrimp-like creatures—in the middle of the open ocean migrate up and down thousands of feet every day. They have special features to help them stay put—to keep them from sinking or floating to the top when they need to stay in one place. Many fishes have gas bladders that help them stay at one depth without much effort. Some gas bladders are filled with fat; others are filled with gas pumped in and out from the blood. Other animals, like squids, swim to stay at depth.

Many kinds of marine animals don't swim, and are attached to the bottom. Relatives of this shallow water sponge live on the bottom of the deep sea miles below the surface.

Many fish in the upper layers of the open ocean look up. Animals above them (like this large jellyfish) are easy to see when they are silhouetted by sunlight or moonlight shining into the water. This diver is adding to the backlighting by using his flashlight.

Living Light

Not only do deep-sea animals live in three dimensions, but they live in dark space too. Below the sunlit surface layer, the sea gets dim, dimmer, and then dark. It is a good place to have your own flashlight.

Here's a shrimp's eye view of a black sea dragon using its chin barbel as a lure. Feel like dinner?

And many kinds of deep-sea animals do! Actually they have what scientists call "light organs." Light organs make a special kind of light called bioluminescence (pronounced bye-o loom-in es-sens). It means "living light."

Animals use living light to find food, to find each other, and to confuse animals that might eat them. Many deep-sea fish and sharks make living light. So do some jellyfish, shrimp, squids, and octopuses. Animals can make the glow of their living light in one of two ways. Some animals have light organs packed with glowing bacteria. Others have cells that make light using special chemicals. Such cells are part of a special organ called a photophore. Under a microscope these organs look very similar to tiny eyes. The skin over the light organ looks like a lens. It can aim the light produced by the underlying skin.

MAKING LIGHT

How do bacterial and animal cells make light? First, it is important to understand that all light is energy. Heat is energy, too, and most light has heat. The sun's heat and light come from swirling gases that are very hot. Living light made by bacteria and animal cells has very little heat and is often called cold light. It is made by chemicals within animal tissue reacting to produce energy. Cells that make living light use a chemical called luciferin (say loo-sif-er-in). The name comes from the old Latin word, Lucifer, which means light carrier. Inside each cell, light energy, and very little heat, are produced when luciferin bonds with oxygen, helped by another chemical called luciferase. Much of what scientists know about the chemistry of bioluminescence has been learned not from deep-sea animals but from fireflies.

The light organ of the coral reef flashlight fish is packed with glowing bacteria.

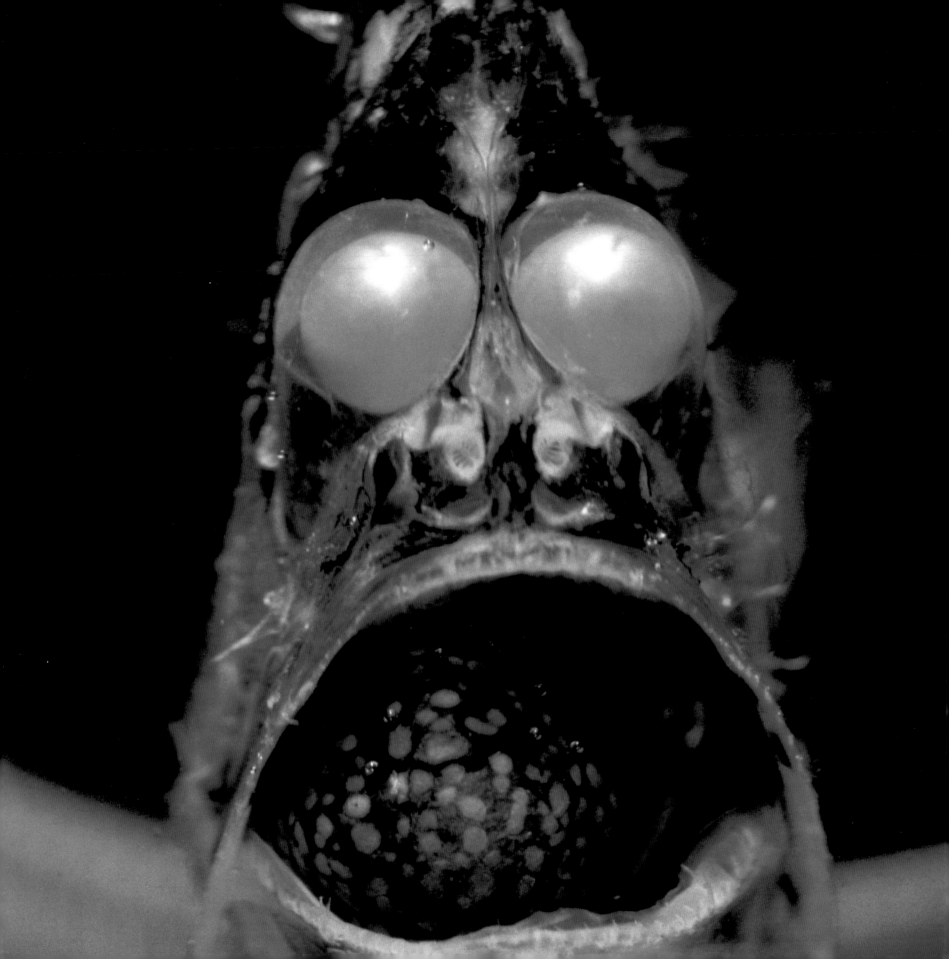

Meet Some Creeps

The animals of the upper zone are the most familiar to us. This epipelagic zone may not seem to be the place to find deep-sea animals, but many of the species found here also make deep dives into darker layers to feed or to escape predators. Many deeper living creatures regularly visit the epipelagic zone, swimming almost to the surface on dark nights. Lantern fish, shorter than the length of your finger, swim almost one third of a mile upwards every night and swim back to the deep in daylight. Lantern fish, as their name suggests, are studded with lights along their sides.

Elephant fish, distant relatives of sharks, live on the sea bottom at least 600 feet deep along the coasts of Australia and New Zealand. They have deep-sea relatives that live miles below the surface.

All of the animals living in the upper layer help to feed the other animals living deep below them. Their wastes and dead bodies drift down and enrich the dark

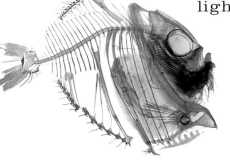

The hatchetfish, whose skeleton is pictured here, lives in the middle layer of the deep sea. These fish have tubular eyes that allow them to look in various directions, especially up.

waters beneath the sunlit upper layers of the epipelagic zone.

Daytime upper zone dwellers include whales, dolphins, tunas, swordfish, salmon, sharks, herring, squids, and jellyfish. Also living here are many kinds of tiny plants and animals, collectively called plankton. Plankton drift with the currents, although they can swim around in small areas. They form the foundation for the food chains of almost every ocean animal.

The first link in this chain of life, the food chain, are single-celled plants that make food using the energy of sunlight. Tiny planktonic animals, the next link in the chain, eat the plant cells and each other. Bigger animals eat planktonic animals, and so on. Even the animals living in the deep sea far below them depend on the planktonic foundation of the food chain. When dead plankton and waste from larger animals fall into the deep sea, they provide food for animals that live away from sunlight.

Animals from the mesopelagic zone, the mid-layer of the deep sea, live in near darkness.

The hunters of the mid open ocean have good eyes. This hatchetfish has tubular eyes specially adapted for looking up.

This specially prepared specimen of a black sea dragon reveals that its lure is attached to its lower jaw.

Many meso-pelagic fishes, squids, and shrimp-like animals have well-developed eyes that are often huge and strangely shaped. Eyes are important for finding food in this dim to dark space. A lot of mesopelagic animals swim up into the upper layers every night to hunt where food is more abundant. This is an area of twilight hunters. In the low light, hunters with good eyes can find prey.

Fishes in the middle layers have silvery sides, well-developed eyes, strong muscles, short jaws, and often big gills. Such features help them survive in dim light and daily swim up for food. Most mesopelagic fishes spend their time looking up. Prey is easier to see when it forms a shadow against the dim glow of light from the surface.

Some midwater fish have silvery sides, glowing bellies, and tubular eyes to help them look up. The silver hatchetfish, a favorite species of the bathysphere explorer William Beebe, has eyes that constantly look up and light organs that point down. Midwater fish, sharks, and squid use living light to blend with the dim glow from the surface. This matching of the background light provides a kind of deepwater camouflage. These shiny surfaces match the light from above and make it harder for another hunter, looking up, to see them.

Hunters in Constant Darkness

No sunlight ever reaches the bathypelagic zone, the deepest layer of the deep open sea. This space is lighted only by the living lights of the hunters and the hunted. Food here is scarce. Hunters move more slowly and very few migrate to higher layers. In fact, most probably move around very little.

The fish that live here have flabby muscles, weak bones, and are colored black or dark brown. They have long, flexible jaws and big mouths. When they find food, they need to swallow it, even if it's bigger than their mouths. A good example of a bathypelagic hunter is the pelican eel, or umbrella-mouth gulper. Living more than a mile deep, this fish, as its name suggests, is almost all mouth. Its jaws are very flexible so it can swallow other animals even bigger than its mouth. Most deep-sea fishes are smaller than a human hand, but the pelican eel and its gulper relatives can be from two to six feet long. Some gulpers have glowing tips on their tails. Perhaps they hang their tails in front of their mouths as lures. No one knows for sure.

Another impressive hunter in the dark is an eight-inch-long monster-like relative of squids and octopuses. Its scientific name, *Vampyroteuthis infernalis*, means "vampire squid from Hell." Even though they live at 3,000 feet and deeper, these hunters have

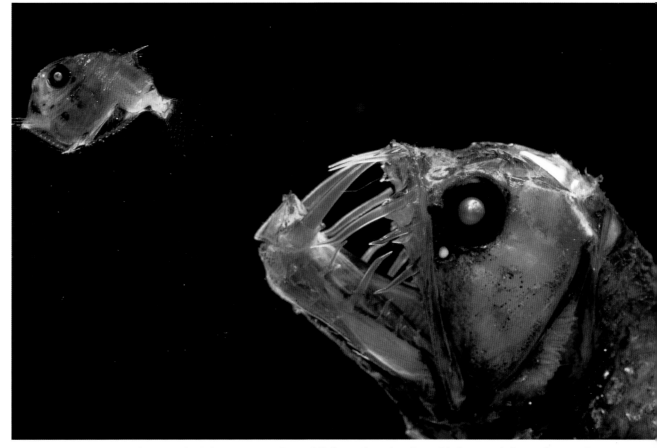

The teeth of viperfish may have inspired the monster-makers of Hollywood movies. Does this face remind you of anyone?

the largest eyes for their size of any animal. A vampire squid smaller than your foot has eyes the size of a wolf's!

We really know very little about how bathypelagic animals hunt. Until recently, biologists thought vampire squid were slow swimmers.

But in 1993, scientists using a remote TV camera saw a vampire squid speed by. They described it as swimming fast, "buzzing around," and doing flips and cartwheels.

Biologists still guess that most deep-sea fish are slow swimmers, but someday, when we finally see them swimming, we may be surprised to find they act differently. Although adult fishes in this zone don't migrate, their young do spend some time in the upper layers of the sea. Deep-sea anglerfish eggs and larvae (very young fish) float to the upper mesopelagic and even the epipelagic zones, because there is more food here for growing fishes. As they grow larger, the young fish travel back down to the bathy-pelagic zone to spend their adult lives.

Although hunters like the vampire squid swim around actively seeking their next meal, others wait quietly and try to lure their living food to them. Anglerfish are famous for attracting their prey. The "fishing pole" of an anglerfish is

ANGLERFISH

Anglerfish, with glowing tips on their fins, use bacterial light to produce the glow. Viperfish have light organs in their mouth and all along their body. The light is produced by the fish itself using special light organs with lenses.

really part of a fin. Anglerfish use this long rod, located over their upper lip and between their eyes, to attract small animals like shrimp. Just as a fisherman uses a fly or lure of shiny metal to catch trout or bass, an anglerfish has a glowing light at the tip of its fishing pole fin. When a small shrimp comes to check out the small light, the anglerfish suddenly opens up its

Deep-sea fangtooths spend their adult lives in the deep sea. But their young float up into the shallower layers where food is richer. The spines on many small open water animals add surface area and help them float and serve as protection against predators.

mouth and the catch is sucked in with a rush of water. Then the anglerfish pumps the water through its gill vents (the hole right below the "arm fins") and swallows the catch. Anglerfish aren't the only deep-sea fish with lures. Viperfish have glowing mouths and a lure on their back, and black sea dragons use a light-tipped barbel on their chin to attract prey.

No matter how a hunter finds its prey, the important thing is swallowing it. Energy is precious in the deep sea where food is few and far between. Big teeth and big mouths are very useful to deep-sea fish, but these features can make them look strange and bizarre to us.

Big teeth, a big body and a light-tipped fishing pole are the hallmarks of many kinds of deep-sea anglerfish.

Life on the Bottom

Hunters can live on the bottom, too. Tripod fishes stand directly on the deep-sea mud propped up on the tips of three fins. Rattails and hagfish cruise right on the seafloor seeking live prey and dead carcasses.

The deepest living fishes include the rattails and grenadiers. Close relatives of codfish, they have big heads, large eyes, and long, slender tails. Below their chins they have sensitive barbels to help find prey buried in the bottom. Long scratches in the deep-sea mud are thought to be made by grenadiers as they plow the bottom looking for food.

Brotulas are small, big-headed, soft-bodied fishes that hold the records for the deepest living fish ever collected or seen. Most of these fish are so little known they don't have common names. A brotula has been pulled up from 23,387 feet—almost five miles down. Perhaps

The shallow water sea cucumbers we see in tide pools and on reefs have relatives that live on the deepest parts of the ocean bottom. Some deep-sea cucumbers can swim.

the deepest living fish in the world is *Abysso-brotula* galatheae (the first name means "very deep brotula," the second name is in honor of the research ship *Galathea*). It was hauled up from the Puerto Rico trench in 1970 at 27,543 feet, the deepest point in the Atlantic Ocean.

But the animal group most common on the seafloor are not fish. They are the group that includes starfish, sea urchins, sea cucumbers, sand dollars, sea lilies, and brittle stars. Shallow water brittle stars, with their coin-sized bodies and long, wriggling, spiny legs, are familiar to anyone who has gone tide pooling. Deep-sea brittle stars are among the most abundant animals at the sea bottom. They live at least as deep as 20,565 feet. Their relatives, the cushion stars, look a bit like a starfish that has been inflated with a bicycle pump.

Sponges are familiar because some live in shallow water but many live on the deep-sea floor in total darkness.

Even deeper—at 32,800 feet—in the same trench live other relatives—deep-sea cucumbers. These little pickle-sized creatures have been described as looking like tiny pigs with strange bumps on their backs. Scientists have found sea cucumbers suck and chew the mud and sand of the bottom to get food. Of great interest to biologists are the few species of sea cucumbers that swim. Some swimming cucumbers look more like jellyfish than the typical cucumber

Some brittle stars live more than four miles deep. Their long-legged spiny relatives are common in shallow water. Look for them on the rocky bottoms of tide pools.

more than 300 kinds of sea cucumbers in the deep sea. They make up almost 95 percent of the total weight of all animals over large areas of the deep seafloor.

Like their shallow water relatives, deepwater shape of their relatives. The sea bottom, where most sea cucumbers live, is as cold as ice. But recently scientists have been studying some hot places on the seafloor in a newly discovered deep-sea world.

A great discovery was made about life on the seafloor in 1977. Scientists working from ships had found areas of the seafloor that were very hot. They decided to use *Alvin*, a deep-diving research sub, to go down and get a firsthand look. They dove almost two miles deep, to the floor of the Pacific Ocean near the Galapagos Islands. Here they found cracks in the seafloor that gushed with very hot water. These cracks are connected to volcanic action inside the earth. Usually the temperature of water in the deep sea is almost freezing. But this water was hotter than boiling.

Scientists were surprised to find white clams as big as a human hand living near the vents in this dark water. Usually, clams live only in shallow water where they feed on tiny plants that cannot live where there is no light.

Curious, scientists made more dives in *Alvin*. They found many kinds of animals living around the hot springs. The most obvious were crowds of red worms living in white tubes attached to rocks. The worms were more than ten feet tall. Scientists were curious about what they ate. These long worms have no gut. Instead, they absorb food directly through the surface of their bodies. But scientists still did not know the source of the food that the worms and clams were eating.

The diving scientists found the answer in the hot water. They found that the water is full of many chemicals, including sulfur compounds. The seawater around the clams and worms was found filled with tiny organisms called bacteria. These turned out to be very special bacteria that can use energy from the sulfur compounds to make food. The deep-sea clams, worms, and other animals eat the food-rich bacteria just like animals in the sunlit part of the sea eat green plants. This newly discovered deep sea world does not need the sun. Scientists have found many lively areas like this on the ocean floor. They call them "vent communities" because they are always near volcanic vents.

Clams that live in shallow water feed on tiny floating plants. These deep-sea clams depend on bacteria for food. © 1993 NSF Oasis Project/Mo Yung Productions

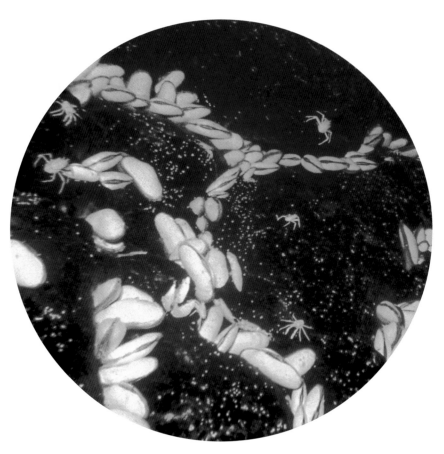

Young anglerfish may hatch near the surface from eggs that float up from much deeper waters where their parents live. There is more food in these shallower waters but there are also more predators.

An important part of survival for any animal is finding a mate. Mates are hard to find in the dark, deep sea. Many deep-sea animals probably find their partners in the dark using their very acute sense of smell. Biologists suspect that female anglerfish may give off odors that float though the water. Male anglerfish sense this perfume and follow the smell to their mate.

Vision, even in the dark, is another way to find a partner. Many fish, squid, and shrimp flash their light organs in distinctive ways or have light organs arranged in recognizable patterns. Of course, flashing lights can attract hunters as well as mates, so this can be risky business. A fish could end up as food while trying to find a mate.

When two animals finally do find each other, they may stay together. For example, when male and female of a few species of anglerfish finally meet, they stick together—literally. The much smaller male bites deeply into the side of the grapefruit-sized female. For the rest of their lives, he will get food from her bloodstream. He can't hunt his own food because his mouth has grown into her flesh. Living his life as her parasite, his only job is to father their children. Other kinds of anglers live separate lives and probably find each other by smell each time they mate.

Adult mesopelagic, middle layer, fish stay in the deep sea, but the eggs produced by the mother and fertilized by the father may float to near the surface. The eggs drift around until the embryo eats all of the yolk. Then the young fish hunt in the rich near-surface waters. Eventually, the young anglers swim back down into deep water to live their lives in darkness.

Many kinds of anglerfish live in deep waters. They range in size from golfballs to volleyballs. In most species, males and females live separately. Only in some species do males attach to females.

Mates are hard to find in the dark, deep sea. When the male and female of some kinds ·····➤ of anglerfish finally meet, they stick together—literally. Look below the tail of this deep-sea anglerfish for the much smaller male (he is about as long as your little finger).

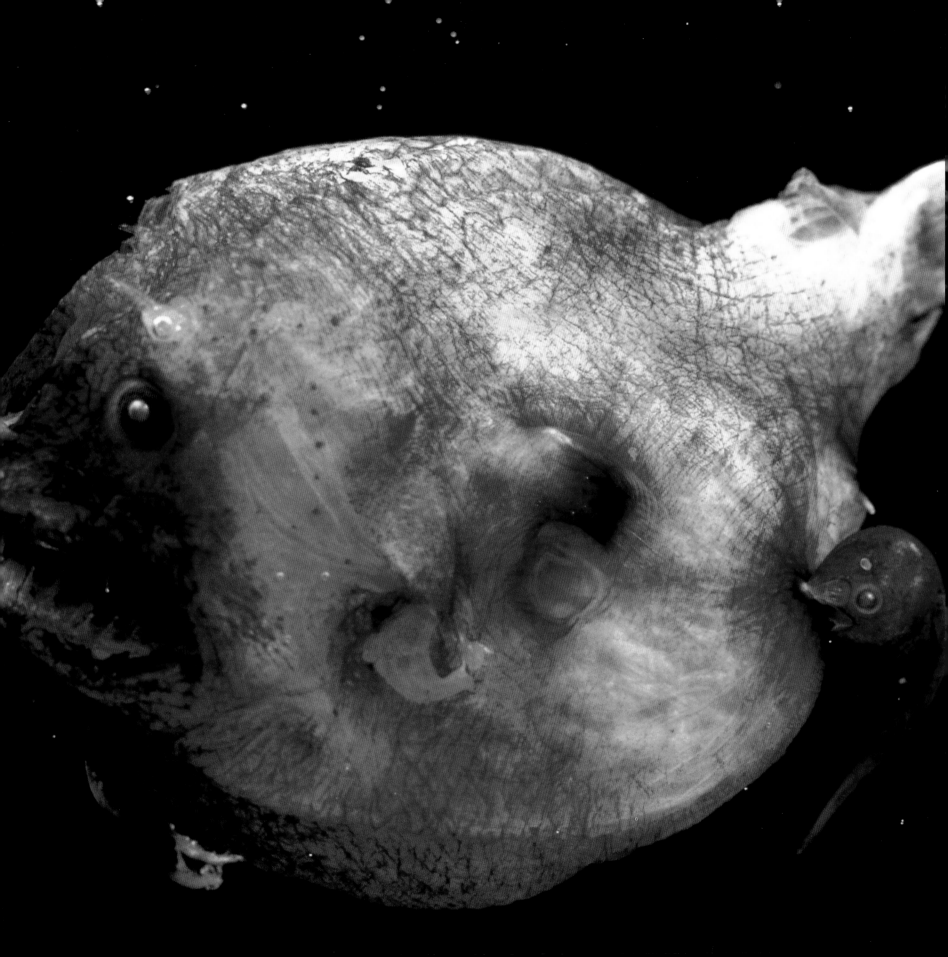

Lots of Legs and Jet-Propelled, Too

The mating of deep-sea animals, as well as other behaviors, are seldom if ever seen. Biologists usually guess about behavior based on what they have seen shallow water relatives do. One group of animals of great interest to scientists is called the cephalopods (seff-alo-pods). These are the squids, octopuses, chambered nautiluses, and their relatives. Much is known about shallow water octopuses and squids, and this knowledge helps scientists to study their deep-sea relatives.

Cephalopods are jet-propelled, have big eyes, and many deep-sea kinds produce living light. Like their relatives, the clams and mussels, squids and octopuses have tubes (also called siphons) to suck in water and then blow it out. By blowing out water, squids and octopuses can jet through the water at high speeds.

They are excellent hunters because they are fast, they can grab and hold on with their suckered arms, and they can see very well. The mouth of a cephalopod is at the center of the base of all its arms. It is equipped with a strong, hard, sharp beak to bite and crush prey like fish,

Once a squid finds food, it needs to hang on to it until it is swallowed. These squid suckers both suck and bite at the same time. Golden brown teeth rim the muscle of the squid's sucker.

crabs, and shrimp. Squids and their relatives are eaten by seabirds, sperm whales, dolphins, and deep-sea sharks, among other species. Biologists

Some octopus live in the upper and mid layers of the ocean, others live on the bottom of the deep sea. All of these eight-legged creatures have well-developed eyes and move using jet-propulsion.

know that squids are an important food for many animals because they have found squid beaks in their stomachs.

Squids and octopuses have long legs, or arms, called tentacles covered with suckers. Often the suckers have sharp teeth inside them. Squids have ten tentacles; octopuses have eight. Chambered nautiluses have dozens of tentacles and a strong, chambered shell.

Most cephalopods are very fast and are only rarely caught in oceanographers' nets. Submersibles and remote television cameras are

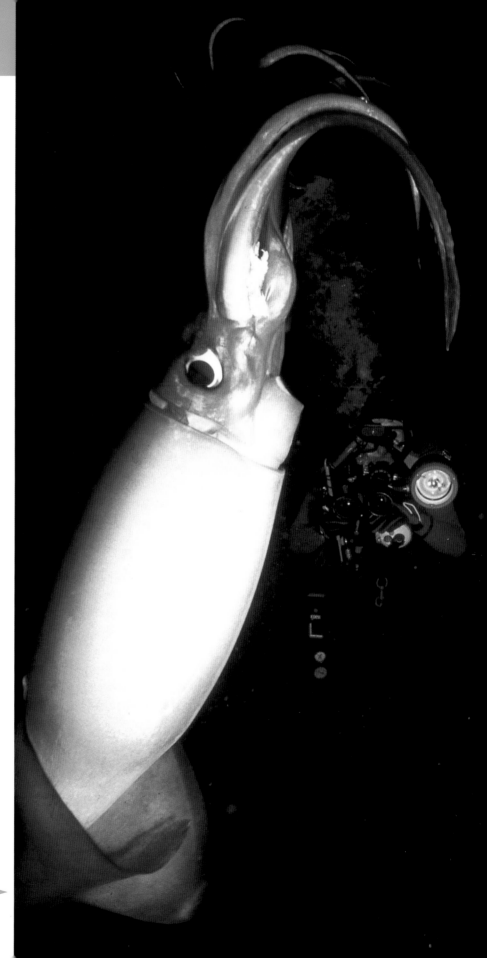

the best ways to learn about their behavior and their biology. William Beebe, in 1930, watched the colored lights of some deep-sea squid from his bathysphere. He was one of the first people to see deep-sea cephalopods in their native world.

In 1954, Jacques Cousteau dove deep into the Mediterranean Sea in a French research sub and saw a beautiful 1 1/2 foot-long squid squirt out a glowing white cloud. Shallow water squids and octopuses squirt black ink to confuse other animals that threaten them. In the dark, deep sea black ink would be invisible, so deep-sea squid frighten predators and prey with their flashes of glowing white ink. There are also many kinds of octopuses in the sea. Some live in open water. Others live on very deep bottoms. Octopuses have been found up to three miles down in the ocean.

Small cephalopods are fascinating too, with their big eyes, fast movements, and patterns of glowing lights. But the most fascinating kind of all is the kraken—the giant squid. Kraken really are giants—they grow as long as fifty-seven feet! No one has seen or photographed a healthy, living giant squid, although in Spring 1997 a research team from the Smithsonian Institution and the National Geographic Society mounted a major expedition to find giant squids off the coast of New Zealand, where fishing boats had caught smaller ones. The squid seekers used a research submersible called the Johnson Sea Link. They had even considered mounting a small television camera (called a "critter cam") on the head of a sperm whale so

Feeding at night in the dark upper layers of the open ocean, this giant Humboldt · · · · · · ▸
squid is longer than a fourth-grader is tall.

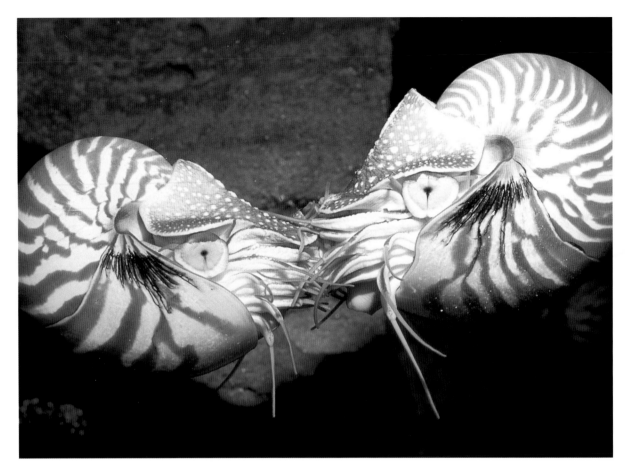

Chambered nautilus are shelled relatives of squids and octopus. In the daytime they swim slowly along the bottom of cliffs off coral reefs about 1000 feet down. At night, they swim up the cliffs to a depth of about 200 feet. Like many deep water animals, nautilus can find more food in shallower water.

of a salad plate, but they are the cephalopods with the oldest fossil record. Compared to their soft-bodied relatives, chambered nautilus are slow swimmers. They propel themselves in the same way, but the heavy shell slows them down. A nautilus shell is divided into many tiny chambers that the animal can fill with gas from its blood. As the nautilus changes depths, the pressure around it changes, too. With its pump system, the nautilus can adjust its buoyancy and neither sink nor float.

In addition to their shells, nautilus have some other important differences from their relatives. They don't have any suckers on their tentacles. Instead, thousands of tiny ridges make their tentacles sticky for grabbing shrimp and crabs. Nautilus have big eyes but they don't have lenses like a squid or octopus. There are eight kinds of nautilus, and they all look very similar. When a nautilus dies, its shell often floats to the surface and washes up on the beach. To hold a nautilus shell is to touch a link with life in the deep sea.

they could see when and if the whale meets a squid. Many people believe that sperm whales eat giant squid.

Little is known about how and where giant squid live in the deep sea so we can only guess. They are probably excellent hunters. Giant squid have the largest eyes of any animals in the world, almost 1 1/2 feet in diameter, about the size of a hubcap.

Not all cephalopods are giants. The shells of chambered nautilus are only about the diameter

There are no plants to eat in the deep sea, so almost everything hunts to live. When most people think of ocean hunters, they usually think of sharks—and there are plenty in the deep oceans. There are more than 350 kinds of sharks. Most kinds of sharks live in the deep sea and are less than six feet long. Many produce living light. Some are so bright they are called lantern sharks. More familiar, shallow water sharks—

Some deep-sea sharks, like this longnose catshark, live on the bottom in waters more than a mile deep. Other kinds of sharks swim up and down in open water.

like the great white, the tiger, and the hammerhead—are unusually large and very different from most sharks.

One of the few big sharks in the deep sea was discovered (by the author) in 1976. As long as a big automobile, this shark feeds by straining animals out of the great mass of tiny animals that migrate up and down in the epipelagic zone. It is one of three kinds of sharks that feed on plankton. The other two kinds are also big and live near the surface—the basking shark and the whale shark.

The newly discovered deepwater plankton feeder has a very big mouth, so people call it the "megamouth shark." *Mega* means "really big" in Greek. Because it swims with its mouth

◀•••As its name tries very hard to show, the dwarf pygmy shark is one of the smallest sharks. It is barely as long as your hand when fully grown. Like many fish living in the deep dark sea, it has well-developed eyes, a well-developed sense of smell and the ability to produce light. The holes near the tip of its snout are paired nostrils. Sharks, like other kinds of fishes, do not breathe through their nostrils. Instead these organs are lined with nerves that can smell a prey fish or shrimp from far away.

Almost all sharks have five gill slits. This seven-gill shark has two more than other sharks. Seven-gill sharks range from shallow water to more than a half-mile deep.

open when it feeds, megamouth was given the scientific name *Megachasma pelagios*, which means "giant yawner of the open sea." Its mouth has many tiny teeth and is lined with silvery skin that reflects the light of shrimp and may help to attract them.

Much smaller sharks, like the cookie-cutter shark and pygmy shark, also migrate, but they have big teeth. Cookie-cutter sharks bite cookie-sized chunks from tuna, billfish, dolphins, whales, and elephant seals.

Many deep-sea sharks live on the bottom. Smaller ones feed on worms and shrimp-like animals that burrow in the mud or flock over the bottom. They have a very good sense of smell and many have good vision. They have well-developed pores on their snouts that can sense the tiny electrical signals given off by the muscles of animals buried in the bottom. One species of deepwater dogfish shark lives as deep as 12,000 feet near the Atlantic coast. One of the smallest sharks, the pygmy shark, is the size and shape of a big cigar.

Big sharks live near the deep-sea bottom, too. A twelve-foot-long Pacific sleeper shark was photographed by a remote camera more than a mile deep. Off Japan, scientists in a research sub saw a twenty-three-foot-long sleeper shark at 4,000 feet deep. One of the largest of all sharks, the Greenland shark grows to twenty-three feet long and lives at least as deep as 7,500 feet. Whether small or big, in deep water or shallow, the 350 different kinds of sharks share at least two things in common—good teeth and successful hunting.

More than 350 kinds of sharks live in the ocean. Scientists are still discovering new ones in all sizes. In 1976, the first "Megamouth" was caught. It was almost 16 feet long. In 1985 two new kinds of deep-sea dwarf sharks were discovered. They are less than 6 inches long.

Deep-Diving Elephants

Not all deep-sea animals are strange and unfamiliar. We can see one kind of deep-sea creature snuffling and snorting on the rocky shores of the California coast. Elephant seals, like humans, breathe air at the surface—but unlike us they can hold their breath underwater for over an hour. It's not because they have big noses either; it is because they have large lungs and special ways of pumping blood to their brains when they swim deep. Actually, the males use their large snouts to show other males how strong they are. Big seals fight to keep areas of the beach for the exclusive use of their mates and pups.

Most kinds of seals seldom dive deeper than a few hundred feet. But elephant seals are definitely creatures of the deep and commonly dive down 1,500 feet. Scientists who study elephant seals attach time and depth recorders to the backs of the seals. The deepest dive recorded for an elephant seal is about 4,100 feet—definitely the deep sea.

Most of their time is spent in deep water. In a twenty-four-hour day, an elephant seal may be at the surface less than four hours. The rest of the time the seal is underwater. It's dim or dark down there, but they do find food—mainly squid. Elephant seals also sleep deep underwater to rest and to avoid fatal attacks by great white sharks. But while they are sleeping,

Big-nosed elephant seals bask on California beaches but at sea they dive almost a mile deep.

small cookie-cutter sharks sometimes sneak up and take small nibbles from their blubbery bodies. Scars are visible on the furry sides of elephant seals and can easily be seen when you watch them on the beach.

Other mammals dive deep, too. After taking a big breath at the surface, a sperm whale can

dive as deep as 3,720 feet. No one has seen a sperm whale diving that deep, but one scientist reported fourteen cases of sperm whales getting tangled in underwater telephone cables. Four of the cables were at least 3,000 feet deep and one was 3,720 feet deep.

It is down there in the cold blackness that sperm whales hunt for their food. They eat many kinds of animals, including tuna and deep-sea sharks and rays, but squid are a large part of their diet. One sperm whale caught by a whaling ship had more than 30,000 squid beaks in its stomach. Most squid eaten by sperm whales are less than three feet long, but it is possible that occasionally sperm whales kill giant squid. Round marks on sperm whales may be scars from the suckers of giant squids.

Whales and seals are mammals, just like us. Mammals feed their young milk and have hair. Most mammals that live in the sea are adapted for deep diving. When we see them at the surface, we need to remember that they also visit the dark spaces of the deep.

Elephant seals are born on the beach and explore the shallow waters nearby. After a few months, they swim to the open sea and spend most of their time diving into very deep water.

Looking at two deep-sea animals—elephant seals and sperm whales—that are known to most people, no one would call these familiar faces "creeps." The deep-sea creatures that are strange and unfamiliar to us are the ones we usually call "creepy." But as you have seen, when we get to know these fascinating creatures, the strangers aren't so creepy after all. Instead, the underwater world is filled with fascinating friends, about whom we wish to know even more. Some of these creatures have only recently been discovered. The ocean has many more such wonders. Maybe you will be the person to discover them.

Sperm whales, like all mammals, breathe air. After taking breaths at the surface, a sperm whale can dive deep, holding its breath longer than an hour.

Last Words from the Deep

This is the end of this book, but we hope it is the beginning of many discoveries for you. Most of what we know about the deep sea has been discovered in the twentieth century. In the next thirty years, scientists will find the answers to many old questions, and they will find new questions to ask, too—

The ocean is big. But sometimes it seems you can hold all its wonder in your hand. This baby sailfish, from the upper open ocean, will share its secrets with those who ask the right questions.

questions that we don't even know yet. It is the job of a scientist to ask questions and to seek the answers. Many of the discoveries to be made in the first third of the twenty-first century will be made by people who are now less than fifteen years old. That may be you.

Now is a good time to begin your own discoveries. Whether you grow up to be a scientist, a photographer, or choose some other career, we hope you will always have a deep interest in the sea.

If you are considering being a scientist, now is a good time to start studying. Read all you can. Some suggestions for reading are: William Beebe's book about his bathysphere adventures called *Half Mile Down* (1934) or *Deep Atlantic* by Richard Ellis (1996). Read books with great pictures of marine life like *Splendors of the Seas* (1994) by Norbert Wu. It also helps to watch television shows and films about sharks, whales, squids, and the ocean in general, and practice using a camera and a computer. Other ways to learn more are to visit or volunteer to work at an aquarium, a marine lab, or a natural history museum.

Remember, all scientists (whether they work in a laboratory, drive a submersible, or use scuba tanks) must have certain basic skills and training. They need to know mathematics, have the ability to talk and write clearly about their results, possess patience and curiosity, as well as have an understanding and devotion to the scientific method. Some kinds of science involve much experimentation and working with equipment in a laboratory.

Many marine biologists watch wild animals in nature. Their results must be recorded carefully, systematically, and mathematically. The study of living creatures, whether in the sea or on land, requires skill and dedication. But take it from us, Leighton and Norbert, it is worth all the effort. Good luck!

Index

Glossary

altitude—vertical distance above sea level; usually measured in meters or feet; also called "elevation"

atmosphere—all the air and water vapor that surrounds the earth and extends from the sea surface to the beginning of outer space

bacteria—tiny single-celled life forms

Bathypelagic Zone—the very deep dark layer of the open sea, from 1,000 meters deep to at least 4,000 meters deep

bathysphere—a ball-shaped chamber with tiny windows and room for one or more people that is lowered into the sea by a cable

Benthopelagic Zone—the layer of the deep sea far from the coast, located just over the bottom and at least 200 meters deep

bioluminescence—living light produced by some bacteria and many kinds of animals by using a chemical reaction

density—amount of weight within a volume

depth—distance measured straight down from the surface of the sea, usually expressed in meters or feet

diadem—a small crown, in the shape of a headband

dimensions—basic types of measurement such as length, height, depth, and sometimes weight and time

Epipelagic Zone—the lighted, open ocean layer from the surface to about 300 meters deep

expedition—a trip organized to discover something or to do a special job

globules—small round drops of a liquid

hemoglobin—the chemical in blood that makes it red, and that carries oxygen

hydrothermal vents—cracks in the bottom of the deep sea from which hot, chemical-filled water gushes out

kraken—giant squid

landscape—the look and shape of a large area of land

larvae—the young, early form of an animal that hatches from an egg

lure—something that attracts or is attractive

Mediterranean Sea—the inland sea bounded on the north by Europe, on the south by Africa, on the east by the Middle East. Its only natural opening is to the Atlantic Ocean, between Spain and Africa

Mesopelagic Zone—the layer of the open ocean from about 300-1,000 meters deep

migrate—to move from one place or location to another

oceanographers—scientists who study the chemistry, life, rocks, and movements of the ocean

parasite—an animal that attaches to another animal and depends on it for food

photophore—a special structure on an animal (like a fish or squid) that produces "bioluminescence"

plankton—tiny plants and animals that float in ocean currents

predators—animals that eat other animals

pressure—continuous force pressing equally on all surfaces; measured in weight per unit area, for example, pounds per square inch

quartz—clear mineral formed from silicon and oxygen

ROV—short for "Remotely Operated Vehicle"; a small submarine (usually with a video camera in it) attached to a research ship or dock and operated by someone on the surface

salinity—a measure of the salts dissolved in sea water

snorkeler—a swimmer who uses a glass faced mask to look into the ocean while breathing through a short tube called a snorkel

submersibles—small submarines used to explore the deep sea

transoceanic cables—large wires lying deep on the ocean bottom that carry signals like telephone messages

trenches—giant ditches or steep-sided canyons in the ocean floor